This Little Hippo
book belongs to

For Emily and Alex
B.S.

For my two fairy princesses
K.V.

Scholastic Children's Books,
Commonwealth House, 1-19 New Oxford Street,
London WC1A 1NU, UK
a division of Scholastic Ltd

London • New York • Toronto • Sydney • Auckland

First published in the UK in 1999 by Little Hippo,
an imprint of Scholastic Ltd

Text copyright © Brenda Smith, 1999
Illustrations copyright © Klaas Verplancke, 1999

ISBN 0 590 19899 8

Printed in Italy by Amadeus S.p.A.

Three Cheers, Charlie Dragon!

by
Brenda Smith

Illustrated by
Klaas Verplancke

Little Hippo

Charlie Dragon was asleep. Suddenly he woke up. He
could feel the rain. He could hear the animals shouting.
"Help! Charlie Dragon, please help us!"

Charlie could not believe his eyes . . . there were no bright
colours anywhere. The sky was not blue. The grass was
not green. All the animals were black and white . . .

. . . and everywhere was very, very wet.

"My goodness," said Charlie Dragon, "what has happened?
Where have all the colours gone?"

"We were searching for Prickles Porcupine," cried Dizzy Tortoise, "when suddenly the rain came down and washed away all our colours."

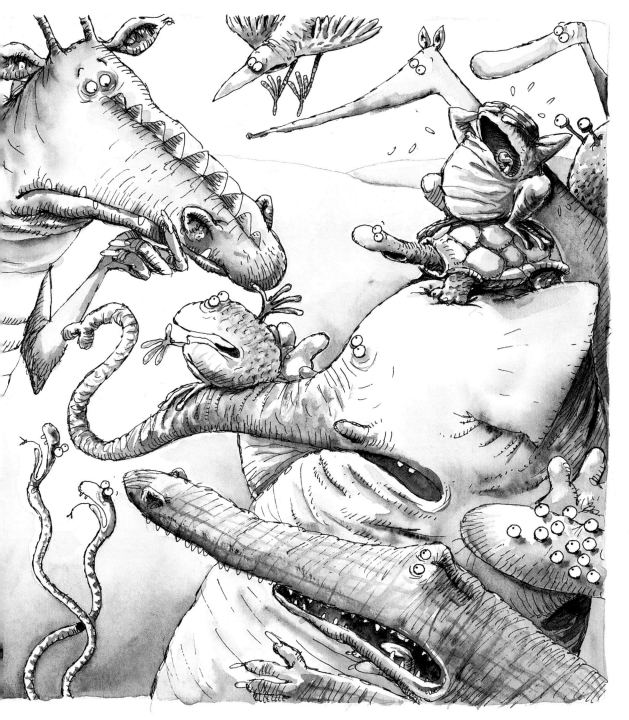

"I should be green!" snapped Smiler Crocodile.

"Look at me, Charlie!" cried Tuska Elephant.

"And look at us!" said Slipping and Sliding, the snakes.

Suddenly, a bright light shone on all the animals.

The sun had crept out from behind the clouds.

A big, bright rainbow appeared.

"Look at those fantastic colours!" said Charlie.

"Yes," said Mrs Nekker, the giraffe, "but the rain washed all *our* colours away. How can we get them back Charlie?"

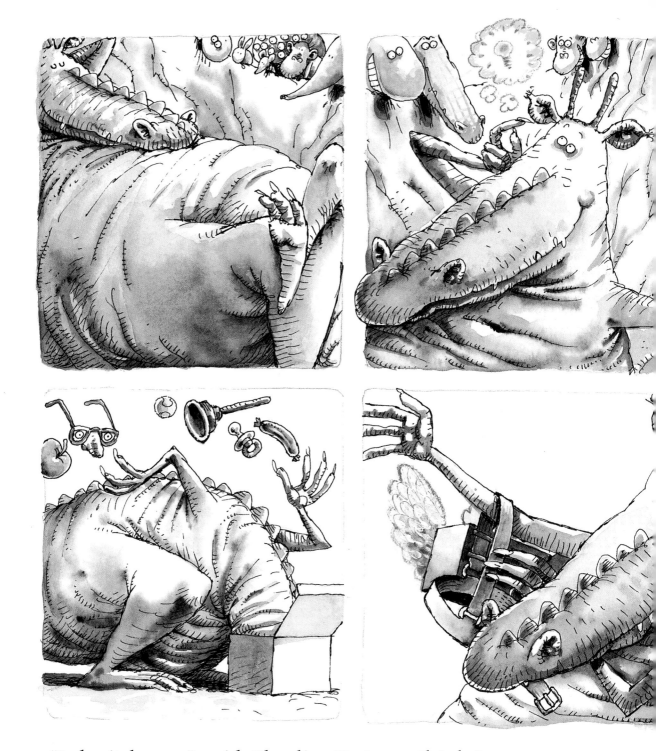

"I don't know," said Charlie. "Let me think."

Charlie sat down to think . . . and fell asleep!

Suddenly, he woke up. "I've had an idea!" he shouted.

The animals watched in surprise as Charlie leapt
into the air. He flew higher and higher until . . .

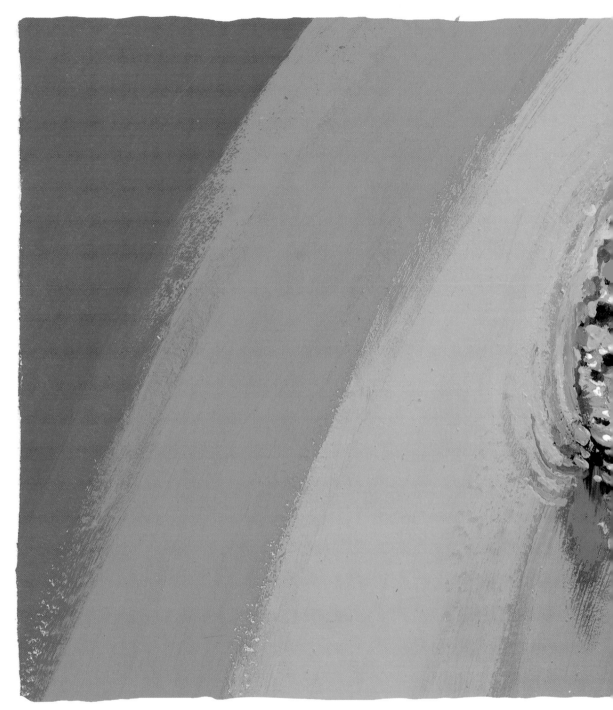

Splash!

Charlie dived right through the middle of the rainbow.

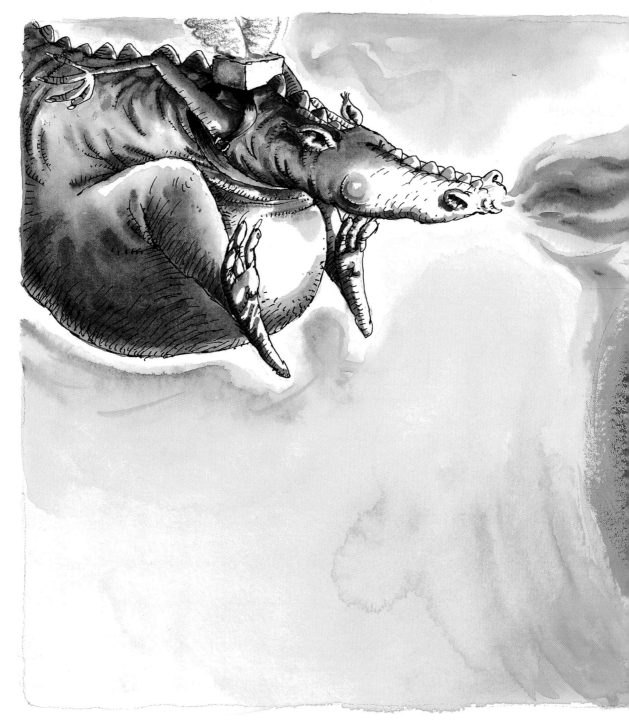

Whoosh! Charlie blew flames on to the rainbow to melt it.

Next, he rolled the melted colours into a huge ball.

Charlie put the rainbow ball carefully under his arm . . .

. . . and flew back to his friends.

Charlie hurled the ball into the air.

It bounced and something magical happened . . .

SPLASH!

The ball bounced again . . . **SPLOSH!**
and again . . . **SPLISH!**
Everywhere the ball bounced, bright colours appeared!

The sky turned blue . . . the trees turned brown . . .
the leaves turned green . . . and yellow . . . and orange.

All the birds and animals had their colours back.
At last, everything was as it should be.

"Well done, Charlie!" shouted Happy Hippo.

"Three cheers for Charlie Dragon. Hip hip . . ."

"What about me?" cried a voice from behind a rock.

It was Prickles Porcupine. He had been missing all day.

Charlie threw the ball to Prickles. POP! The ball burst and
the colours exploded in all directions! When Prickles
opened his eyes, he was lots of different colours . . .

. . . just like a rainbow! "Well done, Prickles!" laughed
Charlie. "You are the brightest porcupine in the land.
You will never get lost again!"

As Prickles hugged Charlie, Mrs Nekker and the
other animals arrived holding a banner which read,
Three Cheers, Charlie Dragon!

Behind them, Tuska Elephant carried a big rainbow cake.

"Let's have a party" cried Dizzy Tortoise.

"Let's celebrate having our colours back!"

"Yes!" laughed Charlie Dragon, "and next time it rains, please remember to take shelter!"

"We will, Charlie!" shouted the animals. "We will!"

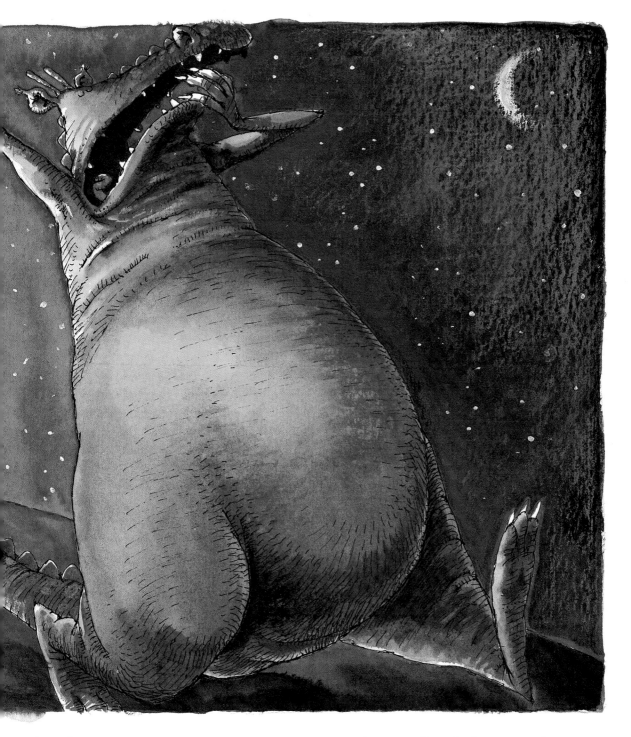

Charlie Dragon ate an enormous piece of rainbow cake
and danced with all the animals. Then with a huge yawn,
he snuggled down . . . and slowly went back to . . .

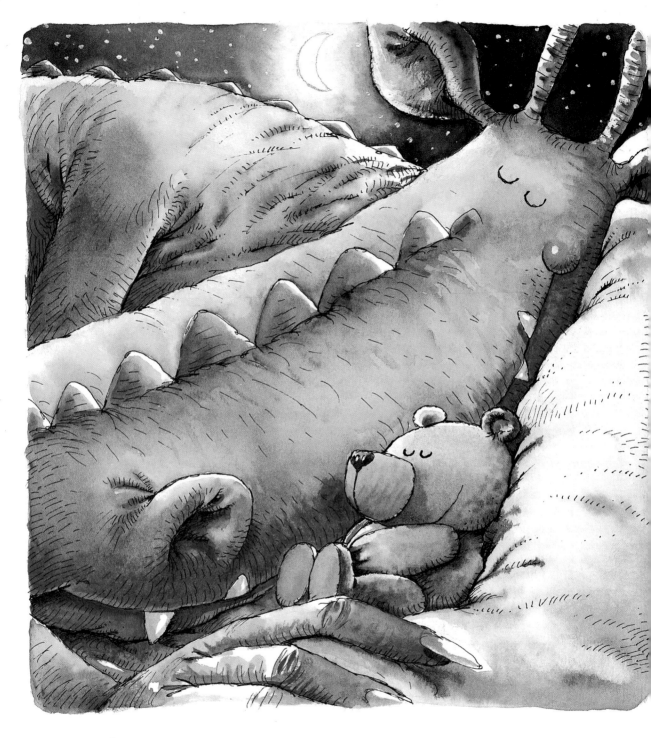

. . . sleep.